Maybe

MW01258281

"With prose that constantly surprises and pleases, *Maybe This Is What I Deserve* is the kind of flash collection that will make you rethink how you see the world. Beneath the arresting imagery of sweaty mashes of bills and noses flowing like gratitude is the heartbeat of an author equally invested in language as character. These stories shock, they entertain, and they stick in your mind."

—Isle McElroy, 2022 Split/Lip Press Fiction Chapbook Contest judge and author of *The Atmospherians* and *People Collide*

"I love Tucker Leighty-Phillips's wild imagination, his privileging of the emotions of childhood, his ability to find the magic that's ever-present in the messiness of community. In *Maybe This Is What I Deserve*, Leighty-Phillips delivers us a surrealism suffused with joy and generosity and wit, grounded in sincere love for Kentucky and for the irrepressible potential of its people."

—Matt Bell, author of *Appleseed*

"In these inventive and open-hearted stories, Tucker Leighty-Phillips takes us back to the most secret, tender moments of our childhoods. He summons worlds where aliens nap in planters, people wait in line for a kiss from a magical catfish, and a monster posts messages to the community bulletin board. Every story in *Maybe This Is What I Deserve*, is a perfect gem I'd like to put in my pocket and carry with me."

—Dana Diehl, author of *The Classroom*

"Donald Barthelme's desire "to be on the leading edge of the trash phenomenon" is spelled out spectacularly in *Maybe This Is What I Deserve*, curated by the edgy midden-minded Tucker Leighty-Phillips. These fictions ping signals, track and reconnoiter, weather weather, and fill the empty space of space with bejeweled juxtaposed junk. They are a flight of cargo planes loaded with asymmetrical language that instructs us to construct these (what?) things even as they (and we) are all falling—shooting stars! smears on the wet windows of cloud chambers! denser diamonds in the dross of exploded diamonds!—to our certain uncertainty."

—Michael Martone, author of *Plain Air: Sketches from Winesburg, Indiana* and *The Complete Writings of Art Smith, The Bird Boy of Fort Wayne*, Edited by Michael Martone

maybe

this

is

what

i

deserve

MAYBE THIS

IS WHAT

I DESERVE

stories

TUCKER LEIGHTY-PHILLIPS

Published by Split/Lip Press
PO Box 27656
Ralston, NE 68127
www.splitlippress.com

ISBN: 978-1-952897-29-0

Cover and Book Design: David Wojciechowski
Cover Art: Eastman Johnson, *The Truants*, 1870,
  Courtesy National Gallery of Art, Washington
Editing: Pedro Ramírez

CONTENTS

"One's memories aren't what actually happened—they're very subjective. You can always make it much better."
        —Wong Kar-Wai

"I prefer not to speak. If I speak, I am in big trouble."
        —Jose Mourinho

DOWN THE TUNNEL, UP THE SLIDE

This is how it begins: your father grants five minutes in the play-place while he orders two hamburgers. You bolt through the door and into the glass room, slip your shoes into the cubby, gaze at the colorful, massive structure towering over you. Up the tunneled ladder you climb, latching onto each rubber rung, dawdling on all fours, fully feral. You rush through each section and subsection, burrowing deeper into the fluorescent caverns. In this place, you are an explorer. In this place, you are an escapee. You rush through a tube, crawling opposite another child heading your direction. You squeeze past one another, giggling all the while. There is optimism here. You are but two cells in this rich, brilliant network. From a window on one side, you overlook the parking lot, where cars pull in and out from the highway, unknowingly surveilled. On the other, you look into the restaurant, where your father is holding an unraveled burger wrapper, bun splayed in two parts, open face and open face, as he shows it to a manager. He has found a stray hair, perhaps a fly. Your father is always finding hair and flies. You, however, have slipped into the heart of the edifice; out of the dense tunnels and into a large room; round, saucer-like, a view of every angle. This is where the children have gathered. You wonder if their parents are finding flies in their burgers too. One boy hunches as the others stand. Soon, he will outgrow this sanctuary. You scan the congregation, this small squirm parade. Into a ball pit you celebrate, dip your hands into the pile, run your fingers across the lining in search of coins, artifacts. This is what your brother taught you. You find something, a dum-dum sucker, an explosive shade of blue. It is dry and packed with dehydrated flavor. You pop the sucker into your mouth, let the artificial berry dissolve, steep your saliva with its richness. Some other child's loss. You drop the sucker back among the balls, let it slip into the pit for another to find; your small camaraderie. This is how it ends: your father knocks on the glass, you whisk down a slide and grab your shoes, return to two legs. The blue still purrs on your tongue.

TODDY'S GOT LICE AGAIN

This is what I tell myself: she'll grow out of it, she's just a kid, it's part of being a parent. This is what I say regarding Toddy, who loves her lice like family. When she's without them, she acts like she's missing a teddy bear or her own birthday party. She rolls in grass the way a dog covers itself in stink, wiggling and twisting until her head becomes a floating hairy hive. You've got to see it. She'll find them in her sideburns, press her middle finger against her skin to trap the creatures, and rather than pinching them out, she'll push them further in, like she's collecting a child who strayed too far from the house. Of course, the neighbor kids don't want to get near her, and the school's sent a stack of letters telling us to take care of the situation before she's expelled, and sleepovers at the house aren't possible because our place may as well be haunted. But the kid's happy. She talks to them, admires them being so close to her thoughts—likes knowing they can hear her secrets. As for me, I'm coping as best I can. Just feels like too many summer days are spent with Toddy's hair styled up with mayonnaise, trying to scare the buggers off for good, knowing it's useless because I can't trust her not to swan-dive back into the tall grass, ostrich her head in the milkweed, tumble into nature a little too sacrificially.

Maybe it's my fault. We're poor, the proper treatment's expensive, maybe she's used to the itching and scratching and bugs bouncing from shoulder to scalp. Maybe she finds it easier to come home to a pillow springing with tiny fireworks, a towel covered in dead like a battlefield, a car seat reminding us these things travel wherever we go. Maybe she's just used to it. That's what we do as humans, right? We find ways to turn our consequences into comforts, to say *maybe this is good enough, maybe this is what I deserve.*

THE YEAR WE STOPPED COUNTING

There was no point to numbers anymore, we figured. Humanity was doomed because we tried too hard to tally everything, to inventory our matters of being. I took a holistic approach to cooking; adding ingredients without measurements. Sometimes my cookies were wet. Others were chalk-block. When Brett owed me money, he gave me a sweaty mash of bills. I passed it back when it was my turn. We were never sure who owed who. The cable company did not appreciate our epiphany, so I set them to autopay. I started reading about the history of numbers. Know your enemy, so to speak. I learned many facts, more than I could ever share, but I was particularly interested in the number zero. Perhaps it offered comfort, the idea of something being nothing at all. But if it were truly nothing, then how did so many cultures come to know it? Each discovering it, naming it, assigning it a value (even if that value was, well…). It had nicknames. Zilch. Nada. Zip. It claimed so much space. This felt like a new epiphany, turning nothing into something. I asked Brett, *what do you think about zero?* and he just kind of shrugged. Didn't feel anything. Nil. I think he was tired of our game. I saw him keeping score during Gin Rummy. Here's the thing: I got a tattoo. A little black oval on my forearm. Told everyone it was just a shape, but really it was an ode. Consider this: zero divided by zero is zero. Remember that when you're feeling low. What a mantra that could be. Whittle yourself until you become yourself. Not even you can stop you. Taking joy in the amount of nothing.

GROCERIES

I've been trying to keep to the outer perimeter of the grocery store. Health websites say it's the best way to avoid processed foods. Most of the good stuff, milk and fresh produce, are along the border. Like a moat, or a barricade. Isn't that funny, all the good protecting the unsavory. Feels like a metaphor. To be honest, I stick to the outside because there's more space. There's less constriction moving around a table filled with peaches than, say, the cracker aisle. There is a sense of drowning among those center lanes. When I see a buggy at the end of one, I think of cage doors. Entrapment. The end of things. Which also makes me think of Jonah, you know, the guy from the whale, or, rather, the guy in the whale. I played him in a church production once. They asked me to do it because they could tell my faith was starting to teeter, cowering from the church bus when it pulled in the driveway, begging my mother to shoo it on from the window. They came back Monday morning and offered me the lead. Jonah ends up inside the fish as a test of his faith, or something. That's how I felt, up on stage, in the center of a papier mâché whale, newspaper articles about high school softball bleeding through the blue paint. The whale was waiting for my re-devotion. In the grocery store, fish can be found on the outer barrier, usually in the back. Salmon, tuna, maybe haddock, depending on region and time of year. Sometimes there's one of those lobster aquariums. When I was a kid, I thought the aquarium was a magnifying glass, and the lobsters were actually much smaller than they looked. Little palm-resting crustaceans. Practically crawdads. I'll never know where I got the idea. Maybe I wanted them to be tiny enough to escape without notice. Maybe, to me at least, being trapped in something massive made you small by default.

THE STREET PERFORMER

When the man grabs me, I am imitating a driveway, a long winding path covered in gravel.

"Take me home," he pleads, his wet knuckles spider-legging my forearms. I try not to react; as a street performer, it is important that I perform a street as appropriately as possible. Sturdy, like a statue, like the Pieta, like a great testament to God; even in the face of lane closure. I am the best street performer, I can make myself incredibly broad or narrow, depending on the scene—but always very flat, unless of course I choose to be cobblestoned, or potholed, which always draws a reaction from crowds, as they feast on government ineptitude. And again, I can stand very still.

"Take me home," the man repeats. The hapless sap is sobbing as he tatters at my arms. I break my hold, bring him to my shoulder. I feel his blathering heart knocking against my own. A car pulls forward and honks at the man, believing he is blocking the street. Sometimes cars mistake me for the actual road and try to rumble over me to get to the boardwalk.

"What makes you think—" I start to ask but he babbles into my sleeve, leaving slippery conditions all along my side, phlegm and snot and tears.

"You look like my childhood driveway," he moans. A crowd is gathering, touristy and curious. Many think it is a performance piece, two thespians playing out an unlikely scenario, a small sidewalk tragedy. A parent gives her toddler a crumpled dollar and she drops it in my bucket.

"Take me back, please, take me home," the man begs.

And I'm forked, my lanes split at the thought of steering away this hurt man, this weary broken traveler. Who is not unlike him, trying to return to their childhood home, or trying to escape it for good? Who is not crooning a song of somewhere else? O fear, to be this man's dead end, but what else have I got? He writhes on the sidewalk, his hand gripping my shoe, clawing my ankle, trying to hitchhike the length of me.

"Please," he croaks. He is rain water funneling down a storm drain. I am an intersection, a roundabout, a cul-de-sac circled by cars with the volume turned down as they try to read each house number. He weathers me and I erode—letting nature run its course as I reduce to something more earthly—and the crowd is hooting, hollering, ham-fisting money into my bucket, and I extend a hand, offer the man a lift, and he makes his way up the driveway, past the mailbox and up the hill, past the row of aging oaks, and together we head home.

STATEMENT FROM THE SILVER-TALONED MONSTER RAVAGING THE LOCAL TOWNSPEOPLE

The Silver-Taloned Monster issues a public statement to the local townspeople, addressing their concerns about his many acts of peeling people's skin like string cheese. The statement is nailed to the community bulletin board, presumably by the monster himself. The townspeople fear The Monster's many ritual killings and flesh-feastings. They're not crazy about the skin peelings. The townspeople hide whenever The Silver-Taloned Monster stomps into the village; taking refuge in their closets, pulling coats like curtains; dirtying their jeans in the crawl spaces beneath broken floorboards; slithering up the roof top to maintain high ground. The Silver-Taloned Monster knows his feastings have become more frequent, his hunger more expansive. He knows the clean, careful cuts with which his talons tear flesh feel almost more cruel than if he were lackadaisical about it. He doesn't have any plans of stopping, but wants to assure the townspeople he hears their concerns. *We're a community*, his statement reads, *and I see you. I'm listening.*

CATFISH WISHING WELL

We are waiting in line to receive a kiss from the Catfish. The Catfish is in a wishing well, and the kiss is not just any old pearl, but a wish. My wish is to become a Dollar General. My children, who are also waiting in line, and aren't old enough to receive the kiss (and as a result, the wish), are in my ear like president's men, trying to give me any other scheme. *Wish to be a country radio call sign*, says my oldest and flimsiest child. My younger keeps pulling my pants leg, saying *bullfrog hurricane, bullfrog hurricane* and when I ask her what such a thing is she says *pretty self-explanatory* and I tell myself that once I'm a Dollar General, I won't have to worry about kids anymore, just fully-stocked shelves and the Christmas rush. Bathrooms mopped every hour. You got time to lean, you got time to clean. The whole shebang. When I reach the front of the line, I ramble up to the corner of the well, puckered all lip up-and-out, waiting to receive the blessing. What's proper kiss-wish etiquette, I wonder. A little peck? Some generous morsel of tongue? The old hand-behind-the-neck? The Catfish has needy lips. It's over before I know it, the wish rolling around like a marble in my mouth. I pluck it from my tongue and it swirls like a mood ring. I stow the sucker real quick, greedy to protect it, keep it hidden from hungry eyes. There's dillweeds in line stretched all the way back to Rockcastle County. This ain't no joke. We walk back and I cup my trophy in my palm, peek it over the edge of my pocket to show the kids, like a baby bird awaiting a worm. They *ooh* and *aah* and I flip a brick in the sidewalk and go ass-over-elbow, spilling my pocket treasure into the dirt. The back of the line goes hog wild dogpile, all groping for my wish, all hoping for a balm. My kids, caught at the bottom of the mound, my poor kids. I try to pull them off. Get your own wish, I beg. Please God not my kids, I plead. My poor kids. Then there's a pop, and from God's intercom we hear it, like wind in the air, a soul singing: *106.2 WCCQ*, and the crowd disperses, and my kids are gone, and so is the wish, and it's just us, me and the dillweeds, and we're grazing to the tune, lauding the broadcast signal, swinging sunny as the drizzle begins, a slimy toad smacking the meat of my back.

MOTHER'S BLESSING

My adult daughter is in town for the holidays with her new boyfriend, a Royal Crown Cola Vending Machine. She directs all dinner table conversation towards him, trying to include him, trying to impress me as we drink coffee after the meal. She says he grew up really sheltered but has changed a lot. *Everyone has room for change*, she says, jingling a pocketful of quarters.

IN SICKNESS AND IN

In the beginning, we illed one at a time. When sickness bit my blood, she spooned me a thimble of honey, made ginger and turmeric tea, swaddled me in blankets like a newborn. When it was her turn, I brought 7 Up, Campbell's Soup, saltines—balms my mother taught me, the only ones I knew. As our love spiked, so did our sick, or perhaps it was the other way around. By summer, we'd both caught it. The affliction settled between us like an armrest. We bought two lovebirds because we were two lovebirds. We made amorous proclamations through coughing fits, French-kissed between our bounty of mucus, made love through fits of sweat until we'd lifted our nausea. We ambled from pharmacy to pharmacy, oozing mucus and fluids like a pair of carnival-sized snails; wincing in sunlight, sniffling in moonlight, faces red and sunken as if sat upon by the buttocks of God. When I vomited the remains of my alphabet soup, I swore I saw the word FATE in the floating pasta bits. She saw last week's vindaloo. Perhaps we were looking at the same thing.

We kept each other close as trash cans and bed pans. Into the toilet we tumbled our Oxyplacerine and Vicobin, our Polylixinol and our Vykinzor, the pills plinking the porcelain and collecting in the small pond of the bowl, each dose a coin in a wishing well. But it was all becoming so much. Our bodies were failing. When the doctor separated us, quarantined us to separate sickness bubbles, we pressed our lips against the nylon in simulation. Our love would only spread.

And then—we were better. Our noses flowed like gratitude, our eyes blinked unanchored by crust or slime. Our bodies had not only healed but grown strong. Immunities like oxen. And then she didn't love me anymore; said we had nothing in common. And I knew it was true, but maybe she'd misdiagnosed, maybe we needed a second opinion. She left the birds. One died the other day. I buried it in a lunch box by the compost pile. The other sits at the dinner table with me. I've named her Lady of the Lake. She sings sad songs. We probably aren't helping one another, but we've got no other treatment.

TOGETHERING

I took a nasty bump on the head and lost the meaning of all language. Don't worry, I'm mostly healed now, although I do have the occasional termite.

The day it happened, I had been put in a hospital. A nurse entered my room and asked if I'd like some jello, and for whatever reason, I assumed she meant she would make my room colder. Objects and concepts rattled in my head, but I could not recall the associative names for anything. Kept putting the wrong plugs in the wrong sockets. I said I would like some jello and the nurse brought me a wobbling pile of what I would have called gumption. The gumption wobbled in its bowl.

"Hi honey," a man who might have been my lover said when he entered the room, "I brought your phone." From this I imagined a long descending tube. Pho-o-ne. Why had he brought me a long, descending tube, I thought.

"May I see it? My phone?" I asked and when he handed it to me I said, "Oh yeah. That one."

He told me I could always talk to him if I was having problems and I kept imagining the small waves that inhabit a rug when a chair or table leg is improperly placed upon it. I was not having those.

I got up to perform the action of a hug to him.

"Give me a, come here," I said. We hugged but I didn't know what to call it so I kept calling it a *together* in my head. I wanted to *together* him. We were *togethering* and he smelled sweet, like a cleaning product.

We togethered for a good long period, his hand rubbing the small plateau of my back like he was collecting its warmth. The hospital smelled and looked clean, yet missing, filled with absence, chock-full of lack. I also felt absent, felt like things I couldn't describe. I tapped my pendulums against my phone and experienced an exploration of muscle memory, the tiny rituals I could recall performing. There were a series of unanswered blinks from people checking in on me. At some point, I would blink them back, but I wasn't quite ready to do it. My phone would perform a tiny coin each time I received a new blink. Whenever a new blink came, the phone chirped; coin, coin, coin.

My Probable Lover removed a board game from his bag and asked if I remembered how to play.

"I thought you might want something to do," he said.

I asked him to give me a rundown, just so I was certain. He pointed and named pieces and cards and sections of the board and my brain felt like a flushed toilet. The words "flushed toilet" weren't in my grasp but the sensation was very present— twirling, gargling, diminishing. I felt diminished, far away, like my brain was at the end of a long hallway and my body were at the other.

We tried to play the game but it wasn't going very well. I knew a few phrases, like *sorry* and *that makes sense* and *oh I promise it won't happen again let's just keep playing,* and I used them often. Eventually, the game was abandoned. The air around me felt buoyant, ebbing and flowing and bobbing me with it.

My Probable Lover nibbled a small section of loose skin from the tip of his something, like he was nervous. When we gazed at one another, I felt a Christmas tree of sensations. Boiling water, an extinguished candle, chalk dusting, the face a dog makes while it's using the bathroom, the smell of a dish in the oven that's certainly gone burnt.

"Do you remember our last conversation?" My Probable Lover asked me.

"I'm not sure I remember any conversation."

Another look. More sensations. A book rained on until the pages were distorted and smeared. Ice melting in a glass of water until it was just a glass of water and the ice was only memory. The flicking of a light switch only to hear the gentle crack of a blowing bulb. These were different sensations.

"Can we," I asked, "Can we together again?"

"I don't think we can," he said. So we didn't.

TICK'S HAIR HOUSE

Tick looked up to find her house had grown a full head of hair. Not just any hair—a well-groomed bob. Just what the place needed, she thought, pulling the rake from the shed to comb her home's new mane. The neighbors, envious of this good fortune, purchased wigs for their own homes in the cul-de-sac; layered bangs and pixie cuts and a mullet for the party house, but Tick took pride knowing her house's hair was authentic, that a strong gust of wind would expose her neighbors' houses as fraudulent. *You ain't fooling me, bozos!* she shouted, clipping one of those new-car-red-bows on her roof's scalp. But Tick's house hair was no match for the passage of time; her home's hairline receded higher and higher up the shingles, past the satellite dish, withered and grayed before falling out altogether. As quickly as it came, her home had gone bald. She regretted lambasting her neighbors, their houses still beautiful and shaggy. The party house at the end had even graduated college and matured to a quiff.

THE YEAR WE STARTED DANCING

There is swing and two-step and ballroom, but salsa is your favorite. When Brett dances, he mutters numbers beneath his breath, counting steps as he shuffles back and forth, trying to keep his feet from fumbling. *One-two-three-four*, he mumbles, over and over, *one-two-three-four*. You tell him not to count, to focus on his footwork. *Haven't we gone over this?* You ask. He is too focused on formulas. He is treating the dance like building a shelf when it should be spontaneous and light. It is supposed to be an explosion of synergy, an act of organic love and passion. Later, you notice Brett counting again, this time at dinner. You make grilled salmon, cooked on low, like the woman on YouTube said. Sprinkled with capers. Squeeze of lemon across the filet. He takes quick bites, counts as he chews. *One-two-three-four*. You catch him again at the theater—an action movie—so you don't hear at first, filtered by the throbbing bass and clanging metal. But during a quiet scene, when the protagonist is saying goodbye to his lover, the lover clinging to a ledge, piloting a crashing plane, waiting for the inevitable end, you hear Brett's whisper, see the fog leaving his lips between sips of cola. He does it again during sex. Counts his steps, so to speak. And yet you continue dancing together, this time a hip-hop exercise class with lots of jumping. A man from a skincare commercial shows you how to twist your body, to bend yourself in tune with the music. It feels like you are playing limbo, a sexy invisible limbo. Brett glugs water. It streams past his Adam's apple. *What does it mean to keep a rhythm*, you ask him, but he just keeps shuffling, waiting for the music to end.

THE TODDLERS ARE PLAYING
AIRPORT AGAIN

They've partitioned everything: the slide is the runway, the jungle gym is the terminal, covered in tiny travelers; anything with mulch is part of the operations area. Nobody flies. Nobody ever wants to be pilot. The toddlers love every aspect of the airport except for flight. Tickle always wants to be the rampie, loading freight onto planes with his sandbox bucket. Dasha is the lav agent, as she's the best at keeping the plane's bathrooms within regulation. Everyone wants to be Bob Mansfield, CEO. They fight over his stock options, shoving one another until you step in and separate them, saying *Lacy, you were Bob Mansfield last time, why don't we let Steve this time?* One child reluctantly plays pilot and discusses weather conditions and itinerary changes with a dawdling crew chief, a snotty kid with both shoe strings loose-a-goose. This is most of their game, quiet discussions, loading and unloading bags into mouths of slides. *This is the fourth time I've been routed through Tampa this week*, pilot child groans while the other begins the aircraft's push back, preparing for takeoff. They bicker over operating the tow motor. When you say, *don't you kids want to fly, just once, don't you want to fly*, they say *that's what everyone thinks on day one, you just come in and fly, no problem, like it's a breeze, you just fly, but we've got an overnighter on a non-movement area and ATC is backed up to Glasgow and I haven't had a single fruit snack today so forgive me if I'm a little on edge, Mr. Sky Cap*, and you step back, remind yourself it's just their game, babble with the other parents, and think of some great taxi propelling you through the sky, vaulting into the blue-and-white, traversing the mighty somewhere else.

THE RUMPELSTILTSKIN UNDERSTUDIES
(PLAY)

This article is about the dramatized performance. For the short story, see The Rumpelstiltskin Understudies (Story). For the original fairy tale, see __Rumpelstiltskin__.

The Rumpelstiltskin Understudies is a play based on a short story of the same name by author Tucker Leighty-Phillips. The play is an experimental retelling of the popular fairy tale, intended to be performed by children who are only given a rudimentary understanding of the plot, creating a semi-improvisational performance.

In his original short story, Leighty-Phillips fictionalized the variations by including a series of attached index cards, prompting the reader to draw from the deck at specific moments, allowing the variations of the cards to represent the children's performance, making the story similar to a cross between a **Mad Lib** and a ***Choose-Your-Own-Adventure*** narrative. In the dramatization, which Leighty-Phillips directed, he only cast children who were unfamiliar with the original Rumpelstiltskin tale, asking them to audition by reading dialogue from ***Willy Wonka and the Chocolate Factory***, and only telling them the narrative events after they'd been selected. The performers were given no lines of dialogue, only the events of the scene, which they were to act out through ad-libbing. Leighty-Phillips was insistent on the children's basic understanding of the premise being the most pertinent factor of the work, even going so far as to encourage casted students to inform relatives and family friends of the process. In some cases, the children were asked to avoid their families entirely, as Leighty-Phillips had created a list of untrustworthy or "blabbermouthed" [1] family members. The director spoke of this process in an interview, claiming that "[children] are cognizant of the world in ways adulthood often undermines...any further direction would strip them of the wonder they bring to the stage."[2]

The play debuted at Cold Pond Elementary School in Occurrence, Kentucky on May 24, 2001, to a sold-out gymnasium, with many attendees curious as to how the story would unfold. The play was performed four times over the course of the opening weekend, before ending abruptly after a natural disaster struck the school, resulting in controversy and the play's cancellation. *The Rumpelstiltskin Understudies* has yet to be performed since.

CASTING

Leighty-Phillips worked with Isadora Lemon, a fourth-grade teacher at the school, to identify cast members. The two had conflicting views over the casting process, as the director accused Lemon of solely recommending students who were troublesome, truant, or otherwise in need of parental guidance and direction, and Leighty-Phillips believed she was using the play as a means of motivating troubled students rather than suggesting the most suitable performers. Lemon, however, claimed this to be untrue, arguing that Leighty-Phillips came bearing an agenda that was not in the best interest of any students, much less those needing mentorship. The pair were able to reach a compromise, as Leighty-Phillips agreed to cast a number of truant students, given the added unpredictability they might offer the performance. He even asked those casted to anonymously write down some of their past transgressions and slip them into his mailbox so that he could find ways to work them into the show. "If they were going to smoke, drink, or steal… wasn't it better to do so on behalf of art?" he supposedly remarked backstage at a rehearsal.

Lemon has spoken about her relationship with the director, claiming his efforts to be "wrapped not in the ideas of children, but that sharing children's ideas was ultimately his idea."[2]

CAST

Although many of the play's casted characters are similar to the original fairy tale, there are variations and additions. The character of the daughter, typically unnamed, is titled Mitsy in Leighty-Phillips's production, as the actress playing her, Mitsy Curl, insisted the character have a name, selecting her own. The role of the Rumpelstiltskin Understudies are also unique to this production. In the casting process, Leighty-Phillips intentionally placed significant emphasis on Rumpelstiltskin's importance in the play, creating a sense of desire among the students.

"He would walk back and forth on stage, saying *remember, Rumpelstiltskin is the star of the show, and everything revolves around our star*," claimed one of the actors.

As a result, the audition process became quite competitive, and many believed Leighty-Phillips's decision to cast Tommy Pepper, a fifth grader who missed two auditions, was intended to be divisive, to create contempt amongst the children, to make them so upset and angry that they'd consider sabotaging Pepper's performance in order to claim his place as their own. After Pepper's announcement, the director also announced that every actor/actress who was not selected for the role would be performing as an alternate for Pepper, and were told to remain side stage for each performance. These characters became the titular understudies. Although the understudies are not technically written into the play itself, their presence looms over each performance, as they are offscreen performers who are given permission to take part should inspiration strike, or if the Rumpelstiltskin actor fails to fulfill their duties as Rumpelstiltskin. The addition of the understudies only further advanced the assumption that Leighty-Phillips was encouraging sabotage amongst the children. A note on their creation features in Leighty-Phillips's original director's notes, as he wanted to increase the likelihood of "orchestrated outside intervention."

CHARACTER	CAST
The Miller	Simon Napier
Mitsy (The Daughter)	Mitsy Curl
The King	Harley McCracken
Rumpelstiltskin	Tommy Pepper
The Firstborn	Lucy Grueller
The Rumpelstiltskin Understudies	Byron Burn, Molly Abrams, Haley Omar, Bryndyn Trinks, Keith Charles, Frida Hardin, Wanda Hardin, Scott Cotton, Blake Sturgeon, + up to four additional performers

DEVELOPMENT AND PRODUCTION

The play was self-funded by the director, although he received financial support through a number of modest artist grants. Cold Pond Elementary was selected as the venue, as Leighty-Phillips wanted to work within the region of Eastern Kentucky where he grew up, and the school was willing to host the play for free, so long as Cold Pond students were cast and proceeds were donated to the school's discretionary fund. Students were also asked to create set pieces, although none had prior experience, and were given complete authority in their design, only being told the basics of the setting ("castle tower" or "farmer's house"). This resulted in students creating a series of decorated poster boards that were

The original set piece for The King's castle, created on standard-issue poster board

too small for the play's stage, misjudging the size of what they were asked to create. Leighty-Phillips insisted on using the pieces. As a result, some performers pretended to be giants, going so far as to stomp through scenes and simulate deep, booming voices as they spoke.

PERFORMANCES

The opening night performance lasted just nineteen minutes, as many of the performers suffered from **stage fright** and rushed through their scenes. Notable moments of opening night:

- During Mitsy's first attempt at guessing Rumpelstiltskin's name, she guessed the names of various **Pokémon**, sparking an impromptu call-and-response between cast members who joined in, naming other characters alongside her.
- Rumpelstiltskin Understudy Scott Cotton entered the stage in the vein of a professional wrestler and challenged Pepper's character to a duel. The scene ended when Mitsy abruptly guessed Rumpelstiltskin's name, banishing both characters. She took a bow and the audience applauded, assuming the play was over.
- The parent of an unnamed cast-member was banned from backstage after encouraging the children to reference a local business they owned during the performance. The business owner has not been publicly named.

The director insisted on not speaking to the cast after each performance, as he did not want to unintentionally sway the actors by offering value judgments on improvised aspects of that night's show. A number of parents and faculty spoke to Leighty-Phillips about the children's continued use of name-calling and insults throughout the opening performance (many children relied heavily on the term "knucklehead") and asked him to ban denigrating names under grounds of inappropriate, impolite behavior. Leighty-Phillips refused, citing that the children were only practicing what they had learned elsewhere.[3]

After the Saturday evening performance, Pepper was replaced as Rumpelstiltskin after repeating some of his improvisations from the matinee show, most notably his choice to perform a number of lines via an impression of the Squidward character from **Spongebob Squarepants**. Rather than committing to a replacement, Leighty-Phillips assigned all of the Understudies to play the title role, replacing Pepper with the nine casted alternates. While performing, the nine new Rumpelstiltskins raced to be the first to deliver a line, or respond to another cast member, or would create factions within the nine to synchronize lines or make inside jokes on stage. One parent deemed this performance to be "unbearable" [citation needed].During the opening of the matinee performance on Sunday, May 26, 2001, the stage collapsed after a **sinkhole** opened in the gymnasium. There were no fatalities or serious injuries in the accident, although many students suffered scrapes and bruises. The play was permanently shut down after Leighty-Phillips engaged in a public scuffle with school officials and the fire department, with bystanders claiming the director demanded the performance continue, citing the natural disaster as "God and Mother Nature's editorial presence." Leighty-Phillips was removed from the property and all future performances were canceled. The play has not been performed since.

CRITICAL RECEPTION AND AFTERMATH

The only published review of *The Rumpelstiltskin Understudies* came from the Saturday edition of the *Cold Pond Gazette*, which claimed Leighty-Phillips's work was "a slice of something straight from New York City, an idea so whimsical and niche that it could only belong to the Big Apple" and claimed the children were "charming, but wholly directionless and uninspired." The Monday, May 25 edition included a follow-up editor's note that claimed the sinkhole was "the unseen hand of a higher power, exposing [Leighty-Phillips] and banishing him back to the big city," but also claimed the weekend's performances had raised over $1,200 for Cold Pond Elementary, enough to buy a new set of Practice Babies and fund the school's Fall performance, a traditional production of **The Three Little Pigs**, directed by Isadora Lemon.

Leighty-Phillips has since fallen out of the public eye. During the filming of *Sinkhole, Kentucky*, a documentary based on the events, Leighty-Phillips agreed to an interview, but one never transpired, as he sent a child in his place.

SEE ALSO

List of Experimental Children's Plays
List of Famous Sinkholes

ANOTHER STORY

After Michael Martone

> *returns from bingo at the warehouse, he finds a chicken in his sun room. This cannot be, Michael Martone thinks. He does not own a chicken. Something's not adding up.*

After Michael Martone

> *discovers the chicken, he aims to capture and release it, but isn't quite sure how. His great-uncle Linus owned chickens in a hand-built coop in his backyard, but they rarely ventured outwards. Seemed like the point. Michael Martone remembers a trick he'd seen where one could tie two chickens together with string to keep them from running off, but that wasn't much help here.*

After Michael Martone

> *empties the trash can, he returns to the sun room and attempts to trap the chicken. This is pretty easy, the can plopping down around the hen. Now, Michael Martone waits. Thinks some more. This is not like catching a bug under a cup, there's no sliding a piece of paper beneath the trash can to hold the chicken in place. How did the chicken even get into the sun room, he thinks. He inspects the windows. Nothing opened, nothing breached. Perhaps the chicken did not come into the house from outside, but was inside the house and is slowly escaping. Had he noticed a chicken in the house lately?*

After Michael Martone

> *opens the door, he lifts the trash can to angle the chicken out, and finds that it has laid an egg. The miracle of life on the floor of his sun room. This is starting to feel like another story, he thinks, one that doesn't involve me.*

MR. BOGGINS

There is a knock on the classroom door. Before Mr. Boggins can rise from his desk to answer, it opens. At the door is a police officer, and he beckons the teacher over. They step into the hallway, closing the door behind them. We look around, inspecting one another, silently beginning interrogations. Is it him, or one of us? We think of the rumors we'd heard, the list of potential suspects. Someone said Josh Manensky had brought a magnet to the computer lab and dragged it across three towers, frying them all. An eighteen-year-old senior had gotten in a fight with a freshman and might be tried as an adult. We had all made salacious posts on message boards, which we'd heard the principal was monitoring. Maybe one of us had taken it too far. Or perhaps it was Boggins himself. A girl in the cafeteria said she'd seen him at Liquor Bonanza buying vodka, and that he was an alcoholic. Could Mr. Boggins be arrested for being an alcoholic? Could the girl in the cafeteria be arrested for spreading rumors? Could we be arrested for wanting Mr. Boggins to be the one getting arrested? William, the class clown, teetered towards the door and put an ear against the glass pane. *I can't hear anything*, he mouthed, but by then, they'd already heard him, and he was in the hallway too.

THE WHIRLPOOL

We thought it'd be a good idea to start a whirlpool, and now Scooter's trapped in the pit of a liquid twister. He's flapping and flailing in the heart of it, arms raised and swaying like he's in the heavy sweat of worship. We didn't think it would be like this when we started, all we figured was if we all marched the edges of Jimmy's new above-ground pool, kept our composure, and didn't let the threat of relief break our momentum, we could make a whirlpool form in the center of the water, a little twirling zipper funneling downwards into some underwater portal. The other games had exhausted themselves, or we'd exhausted them, shouting "Polo" into the air while zombie-treading, barreling rubber torpedoes into legs and crotches, diving to the bottom to snatch batons and coins, lifting our goggles upon re-entry and feeling the suction squeeze of the water wading in our noses. Those were all fine, but the whirlpool, now that was something. Little did we know Scooter would fall into the center, his legs ensnared in its swirling grasp, pulling him down into the drain of itself, forcing him to wheeze a plea to be saved, making him beg for help, making him choke. We didn't want to leave him there, but shit. Mitzy was on the deck, eating a lipstick-colored popsicle like she was sucking the mercury from a thermometer. Jimmy shouted, said it was too late for Scooter, and we watched his body drain, witnessed the ghostly choke of his tummy flab against the wet cotton of his swimming shirt, the way his fingers pulled like telephone wire towards the ladder, or me, or anything beyond the flush.

EVERY GOOD BOY DOES FINE

One day, Ms. Packer gets frustrated with Benjamin and places a refrigerator box around his desk. *You're staying in there until you get your act straight,* she says. After that, we don't hear from Benjamin for a while. Ms. Packer writes music scales on the board. E-G-B-D-F, she writes. *Every Good Boy Does Fine.* That's a way to remember it, she tells us. She brings in a cart with musical instruments; bongos, recorders, maracas. She passes them out at random. We bang on our instruments, blow in them, rattle them. Class is fun. We make lots of noise, more noise than Ms. Packer has ever let us make, or any other teacher, for that matter. There is no noise from Benjamin's box. She writes on the board again. A-C-E-G. *All Cars Eat Gas,* or *All Cows Eat Grass.* Pick one, she tells us. We like to remember things in this way. It makes memory a little game, thinking of those cows in the field, all the good boys in the world. Benjamin doesn't get an instrument, but at the end of the day, Ms. Packer lifts the box from around him, ending his sentence. She places the box in the corner behind her desk, says she'll save it in case she needs to use it again. They stare at one another, both making a tremendous noise the other cannot hear.

TECHNOLOGIES

When I was a boy, I impersonated DVD menu screens for other kids at school. They gathered in the hallway between classes. Someone called out a movie, passed a dollar my way and incited the performance. I'd replicate menu music, mimic three or four repeating quotes, perfectly time the abrupt pause before looping to the beginning, complete with a sharp stunted body motion. I was a track skipping upon myself. The act was a hit. The library knew my scent, watched as I carried stacks of flicks I never watched, only studied. Lunch money rolled in. All the Yoo-hoo a boy could imagine. I won the talent show by performing my own History of Film, from *39 Steps* to *Toy Story 2*. The gig transcended the schoolyard. I started performing at flea markets, outside the doors of Wal*Mart opposite the scout cookies. Someone asked for *The Matrix*, so I made myself a fax machine, a choral chant, the blister of gunfire. For *Home Alone*, I became jingle-belled and melancholy. Sometimes I bluffed. *Terminator 2* was a mystery to me, but I clanked metal and gritted teeth anyway, and the gentleman tipped me a five. Occasionally, an older person would request an antique movie, one of those Big Lots films with a single restored release, the menu all but a still frame. I became a low-budget affair. Quiet and remembering. Eventually, the well dried, requests stopped coming. Sometimes the neighbor offered me a few bucks to make something to fall asleep to. Folks found new forms of entertainment. Nobody wanted to wait around anymore. Everyone wanted to press play. Even later, I renaissanced, became a reason to look back, but that didn't last long, either. Everything loops around in that way, I guess.

THE HOLLISTER STORE

Millie and I stood in the foyer of the mall gawking at the entrance of the Hollister store, thinking about how it looked like a party we hadn't been invited to join. There was music percolating within, deep within, like it was in a back corridor of the space, pillowed by doors and walls, enjoyed only by preferred guests. Millie, older than me and in high school, says she went in once, compared it to a haunted house. "There's this fog coming from the doorway, you know," she said, clutching her Old Navy bag, filled with discount blouses and blue jeans, "and it's all dark and you can't quite tell where anything is. I stumbled backwards into an employee who said nothing, just stared down at me and gave me a look like I should leave." We peered at that Hollister store like it belonged to some miser at the top of a hill, like there was nothing but evil lurking in its walls. We both wanted to peek in so badly, drop our bags of clearance American Flag shirts, smell the rich perfume of the mirage-like California sensibilities, press our faces against the expensive cotton polo shirts and parka jackets. But that wasn't who we were. We wore hand-me-down underpants with our older cousins' names sharpied into the buttocks; our shoes came from an outlet store at the other mall; our spirits felt as reduced as our school lunches. We didn't even really like the clothing, the heavy branding across the chest, phrases like SURF and CALI scrawled down sweatpant legs—but for a moment, we set down our bags, took a step through the cinnamon bun musk of the mall, felt the bass of the looming dance pop beating in tune with our own devices, and imagined what it meant to wear one of those shirts, how it might feel against our chests, what else could be imprinted on its heavy fabric.

CLEM'S SECOND REFRIGERATOR

I had never spent the night at Clem's house before, but I felt the spirit swelling within me the moment I rang the doorbell. The erupting song from the button was warm and welcoming, the rhythm of the bell warbled "we're / so / happy / to have you / join us," whereas my screen door had a human alarm, one which often shouted *Shit or get off the pot, you're letting all the good air out.* And when Clem asked if I wanted something to drink, and I said yes (because of course), he said, "Come with me," and directed me through the den and towards the garage. From there, he unveiled a shrine, an unthinkable bounty. In the garage was a second refrigerator, and when the door opened it shined like the holy grail. On each shelf and crisper cabinet was a splendor of beverages. Capri Sun and bottled water and Snapple and a twelve pack of beer (don't even think about it, he said) and A&W Root Beer and Vanilla Coke and drinks I'd never seen. How did anyone choose anything at all? How could they? At my house it was water, or if you were lucky, Kool-Aid.

That night, I lay on the bottom bunk of Clem's bed and bobbed in a state between dream and longing. The way the light bloomed from the fridge, the choke I felt when I saw the treasures it held. Clem had no idea, gave no second thought as he snatched a blue Gatorade from the side door. I felt my body mop over with some hot red soap, some sticky sensation of anger. If that were me, I'd be at the fridge like an altar, on my knees with the door open, letting the light glaze over me like a cloak in the cold dim dark of the garage. I would take from it, fill a tub with the endless bottles of Sobe fruit drink and baptize myself in its offering, singing and giving praise to the wonders offered to us from the glory. From door to door I would spread the good news, visit those on their last Kool-Aid packet, their final scrape of sugar at the bottom of the bag, and I would say, "Blessed are the meek," as I offered them cans of cola and bottles of expensive island spring water. If the refrigerator had feet, I would kiss them, wash them, sing them a hymn, speak in the tongue of the device's steady vibrating hum until my salvation was quenched.

STAGES OF GRIEF

(co-written with Rachel Reeher)

I get upset and hit my little brother. Naturally, he cries, a feeble sob that works itself into a full-on tearful roar. *I didn't even hit you that hard*, I say. We were playing a game, or at least I thought we were. Now he's all snotty. I try to shush him, grip his elbow, tell him to stop. *We'll both get in trouble*, I warn him. Footsteps slug down the hall towards our room. My brother keeps going, wheezing heavily, and my attempts to quiet him only exacerbate the wailing. I bargain with him, offer baseball cards, wrestlers, and candy if he'll quiet. He shivers and sniffs, works it out in his little mind. He points at the Big Boss Man. My favorite. The keystone of my collection. The door-knob turns. A smile unfolds across my brother's face. He takes the figure in his hands, the terms of my surrender.

GAVIN AND MERLE ARE ENGAGED
IN A TURF WAR

over the parking lot of Aldi's. They bustle to snag unattended shopping carts, return them to the carousel, accept the quarter deposit from the locking mechanism. They position themselves like athletes or secret service agents, waiting for an old blue-hair to leave her cart in the parking spot as she pulls out to head home. Last year, the pair land-battled over the road-side aluminum on Golley Road, where they both trash-bagged Mountain Dew cans to take to the Burp-O recycling center. Gavin's Dad says Merle is trailer-park-trouble. Gavin's family lives in a trailer park too, but a different one. Nicer, his dad claims. At least they don't leave Christmas decorations up all year long. That's tacky, his dad claims. Gavin and Merle's parents work for the same call center, where they're paid on commission and a complicated series of metrics. They both have a script they must adhere to, repeating the same pitches and assurances as their supervisor listens on their calls. Gavin and Merle fight in the Aldi's parking lot, which upsets the balance of the business, because Aldi's is kind of the pastoral grocery store; the gentle alternative to supercenters. Maybe now that boy will get a real job, Gavin's dad claims. A week after the fight, an attendant is assigned to gather loose buggies, and they're not allowed to keep the quarters.

MIDGE WOKE TO DISCOVER SHE'D BECOME A LIGHTNING BUG

on the day she was supposed to play Violinist #2 in her high school the-ater's rendition of *Titanic*. Not quite a lightning bug per se, she didn't have wings or anything, but she had grown a large translucent pouch that ex-tended from the small of her spine to the back of her knees. The pouch glowed rhythmically and when she pressed a finger to it, she found it fatty and gelatinous. This was no thing for a teenager to have, she thought, and imagined scenarios of other students teasing her. Boys flapping about her like moths. Midge, in bed, anatomy flickering like a television left on. No thing for a teenager to have. This would leave her no choice but to abandon the flight of society, head to the hills, find other fireflies dancing and blinking above the switchgrass of a secluded field, all swinging and swaying their pouches like that scene from *The Sound of Music* (which she hadn't seen but knew enough about), and she thought maybe that's what she needed, a community of equitable beings, where no one fussed what brand of shoes they owned or how slim their ankles were, they just dallied through the air, blinking and glowing. Maybe that's what she needed after all, Midge thought, maybe this was best. That evening she was dropped from *Titanic*, as the crowd kept mistaking her for a lighthouse.

WOULDN'T IT JUST BREAK
HER DEAR OLD HEART?

After Adnan's dad died, he started blowing big chewing gum bubbles behind me in Civics. His father had bought him a pack of Fruit Stripe every
morning when he was alive, and since his passing, Adnan chewed the stuff
furiously. Piece after piece, smacking his wet lips as he slurped the flavor
from each strip. Every time he slipped a new piece into his mouth, his
wad got heavier, his bubbles grew larger, narrowly missing the back of my
head as they popped and deflated. I tried to be kind when I asked Adnan
not to blow his bubbles so close to my head, but he kept at it. Just packed
his cheeks and pushed. I don't think the others knew it was related to his
Dad's passing; I don't think the others thought about it at all. It wasn't their
head in his bubble. If I'd been a little girl, adults would've said Adnan was
flirting with me. I didn't think that's what it was. I felt bad about Adnan
and his Dad, but I didn't want his gum in my hair. Everyone said I had
my mother's hair; long, curly at the bottom, a deep earthen brown. I liked
my long hair. It made me feel like a skateboarder. My mom used to give
me bowl cuts. Dreadful ones. She wanted to save money, making me look
like a little shag lamp. Whenever Adnan snapped his bubbles in my ear, I
thought of his Dad, what it meant for Adnan to have something of his to
savor. This is why I tried to be patient, inched my desk forward with my
feet, made space between my head and his clumsy smacks. This was all I
could do: let him blow his bubbles, pull my mother's hair over my shoulder,
and listen, listen, as he breathed air into the only thing he had left.

TUCKER LEIGHTY-PHILLIPS 2: THE SEQUEL

After a successful crowdfunding campaign, the studio announced the production of Tucker Leighty-Phillips 2. The original maintained modest cult status, primarily amongst those in trading card shops and online message boards, but had seen a plummet in popularity due to the increasingly dated style of humor and visual effects. The Original Cast was not brought back for the sequel, with the studio opting to go a different direction. The Original Cast pinched silver hairs from their beard and worked the convention circuit, signing black-and-white 8x10 photographs, snapping selfies with eager fans, pulling the promoter aside to ask if they had a couch The Original Cast could crash on for the night. The couch was comfortable, a sturdy sectional, but coated in dog hair. When The Original Cast awoke in the night, they felt a hair tickling the space between the back of their tongue and entrance to their throat. The hair was too far to pinch with their fingers, and they felt the only recourse was to swallow the hair, but despite their best efforts, they could not get the hair to go down. Sometimes, The Original Cast stops at a roadside attraction, the type of tourist trap where a mummified armadillo sits posed behind a curtain for a five-dollar entry fee, and The Original Cast hands over a bill, waits for the owner to recognize them. Roadside tycoons always do. The Original Cast holds the bill in their hand, waits for the eye contact, holds for a response, and again they feel the hair in the back of their throat, feathering their gag reflex. They feel the lurch of what they can't yet swallow. The grip a body holds on itself. The power of such a small thing. A release date has not yet been announced.

THE ALIENS

The children are standing very still, so as not to upset the aliens. If the aliens see them move, if they turn to watch the children as they advance the footpath or climb the steps to their back porch, it's all over. They must start again. They must be careful. They do not want their game to end. There are nearly a dozen aliens, many taken in as strays, found abandoned in cardboard boxes outside of parking lots, nurtured runts from previous litters. The easiest alien to sneak past is Boots, who sleeps through most of the day, curled in one of the large outdoor planters. Purcell is the most difficult to fool, as she patrols constantly and has a tendency to chase birds, other aliens, the children. But today, the children are standing very still. They are tiptoeing the new terrain, silently recording data, taking soil samples from the backyard as they keep a close eye on their oxygen levels. The children track each of the aliens; noting when they laze on the cold stone porch, nestle between the curtain and the window, defecate in the tall grass of the yard. *Perhaps a religious ritual*, one notes. When threatened, the children stand very still. They do not want their game to end. They sketch drawings of new specimens, bring them to home base for further study. When an alien crosses their path and lays in the driveway, gathering sunlight on its alien skin, they slip over the side railing. They are careful. They are learning. They do not want their game to end. When an alien enters the garage while the children refuel, they hold their breath and wait for it to slink off. They are careful. They are learning. They do not want their game to end. When their father comes home, slamming the door behind him as he bellows, sending the aliens scattering across the house and yard, the children slip out the backdoor. They stand very still. They wait for the sound of the television, for the moment to pass, to slip out into the magic hour. They are careful. They are learning. They do not want their game to end.

ACKNOWLEDGEMENTS

Stories (or versions of these stories) in this collection first appeared in the following journals: *Cheap Pop*, *Sundog Lit*, *Tiny Molecules*, *HAD*, *X-R-A-Y*, *Sporklet*, *Pidgeonholes*, *Post Office Box*, *Fractured Lit*, *Passages North*, *elsewhere*, *Obliterat*, *BOOTH*, *The Journal*, *Pithead Chapel*, and *Wigleaf*. The story "The Rumpelstiltskin Understudies (play)" features an illustration by my sister, Camille Lawson.

I am eternally grateful to the entire team at Split/Lip Press; Kristine, Pedro, David, Caleb, Emmy, Isle McElroy, and the readership team for believing in this collection. I'm thankful to all of my mentors—Matt Bell, Tara Ison, Joe Scapellato, Rick Rinehart, GC Waldrep, Elena Machado, Rob Rosenberg, Mai-Linh Hong, Casey Bohlen; all of whom eased my nerves on a consistent basis, talked me through ideas, and supported my long-term success. I cannot express enough how thankful I am for everyone from my MFA program—I couldn't imagine a better group of people to help me develop as a writer, educator, and human being. And to the great community of writers beyond grad school—Ben, Emily, Lauren, Evan, JJ, Dana, Lindy, Rhea, Jacob, Robyn-Phalen, Cammie. Y'all have sharpened my mind and writing significantly, and I'm thankful to be friends with each of you.

This book was written with additional support from the Art Farm, The Tin House Writer's Workshop, Craigardan Farm, and the Virginia G. Piper Writer's House. Thanks for giving me time and space to write!

To my best friends—Travis, Zach, and Kyle. Y'all have seen me at some really low points. Your friendship helped bring this thing to life and kept me alive as well.

This book is also for Carmen Gillespie. You and I once visited a tree that was so old it only bore rotten fruit. You joked, said we should compete to see who could put that image into a book first. Here it is: that tree is part of the topography of this collection, but its fruit is fresh, mouth-watering, and abundant. You are there too—sitting beneath it, book in hand, lively as ever. There are no dying fruits here. I miss you dearly.

To my sisters, Molly and Camille. You are both wonderful, and kind, and thoughtful. I am fortunate to have grown up alongside you both.

This book, in many ways, is for my mother. You have always supported my vision, even when there was reasonable cause not to do so. You sent me money when you had none. You offered me love when you needed it yourself. I am a community-minded person because you made me one. Thank you for making the world a better place.

To Rachel, my life was static before I knew you. Now, every day is music. I love you and look forward to many more years together.

TUCKER LEIGHTY-PHILLIPS is a writer from Southeastern Kentucky. He is a graduate of the MFA in Fiction program at Arizona State University His work has been published in *Booth*, *Adroit Journal*, *The Offing*, *Wigleaf*, and elsewhere. He has been anthologized in *Best Microfiction* and received a Notable Mention in *Best American Sports Writing*. Before writing, Tucker was a tour manager for a number of punk bands—spending much of the year traveling across the country. Currently, he lives in Whitesburg, KY. His website is TuckerLP.net.

NOW AVAILABLE FROM
SPLIT/LIP PRESS

For more info about the press and titles,
visit us at www.splitlippress.com

Follow us on Instagram and Twitter: @splitlippress

Printed in the USA
CPSIA information can be obtained
at www.ICGtesting.com
CBHW021318081024
15564CB00014B/145